IAIN

A Highlander Romance
Book 19

The Ghosts of Culloden Moor

Melissa Mayhue

Published by Melissa Mayhue
Copyright © 2016 Melissa Mayhue
Last Updated - 02/2016
Cover art by Inspire Creative Services

The Ghosts of Culloden Moor Series
© 2015 Lesli Muir Lytle

All rights reserved.

Print Edition ISBNs:
ISBN-10:0989827291
ISBN-13:978-0-9898272-9-4

Ebook Edition ISBNs:
ISBN-10: 0989827283
ISBN-13: 978-0-9898272-8-7

A NOTE ABOUT THIS SERIES:

Although the individual stories of Culloden's 79 need not be read in strict order, the first book in the series, *THE GATHERING,* should be read first so that the reader fully understands what's going on between the Muir witch and the Highland warriors from 1746.

THE RECKONING, Number 79's story, will finish up the series.

The names of Culloden's 79 are historically accurate in that we have used only the clan or surnames of those who actually died on that fateful day. The given names have been changed out of respect for those brave men and their descendants. If a ghost happens to share the entire name of a fallen warrior, it is purely accidental.

You can find a list of all the stories so far at the series website:

www.ghostsofcullodenmoor.weebly.com

To learn more about the series or to chat with other readers, you can visit the warriors' Facebook page:

www.facebook.com/GhostsofCullodenMoor

OTHER BOOKS IN THIS SERIES:

GHOSTS OF CULLODEN MOOR
Authors as noted
Series Developed by L.L. Muir

ACKNOWLEDGMENTS

My sincere thanks to series creator, Lesli Muir Lytle, for allowing me to be a small part of this wonderful project.

PROLOGUE

Culloden Moor
April 1746

The bullet piercing the flesh of Iain MacIntosh's back came as no real surprise. He'd never been much of a fighter. Even when the lads would gather outside the stables to share a wee dram, Iain had never been one to engage in the fisticuffs or feats of strength. He'd been the one to sidle into the shadows and watch the revelry from afar.

But after the beautiful lady Anne had paid her visit, even a peaceful man such as Iain had proudly marched out with his cousins, making their way along the path that led eventually to Culloden Moor. Their hearts filled with love of kin and clan, their chests inflated with confidence in Prince Charlie's God-given right to rule, they'd marched on, like lambs to slaughter.

No, the surprises of that gloomy April day in 1746 had come later. The first arrived when Iain had realized that the Prince in whose name he'd fought had abandoned those like him, the wounded who lay stranded on the battlefield. The second surprise had come in the form of their enemies' callous disregard for life.

Unable to move more than his arms, Iain had spent the better part of his conscious hours torn between cursing his Prince and praying for some miracle to save him. He thought those prayers answered when a booted toe prodded at his shoulder and a pair of hands flipped him over onto his back.

"This one yet lives," his would-be savior called out.

"Not on our watch, he doesn't," another answered.

This was what their faith in Bonnie Prince Charlie had brought them to. An ignominious death in a sodden field. Alone. Abandoned.

Iain hadn't the strength or the time to protest as the musket rested against his head and discharged. He had only the seconds to curse the Prince one last time, with his final breath.

CHAPTER ONE

Culloden Moor
Present Day

"Ye' were called Iain, were ye' no'?"

Soncerae, the beautiful young witch, waited for his answer, her eyes filled with an emotion that could be either sorrow or pity. Iain couldn't be sure of which, though he liked the idea of neither.

What he was sure of was that he didn't completely trust the dark-haired beauty. True, she'd always seemed nice enough. Just as it was true that they'd all of them, all seventy-nine of them, been drawn to the lass from her first visit to Culloden as a mere babe in arms.

But things had changed with her latest visit. This time she'd come offering the revenge they all hungered after and all they had to do to reach that long-desired goal was to perform a simple task for their little witch. A quest of sorts. The thing was, the men who had risen and gone on Soni's mysterious quests had not returned. Iain wasn't sure what had happened to them, but often enough, not

3

knowing was more frightening than facing the whole of the English army had ever been.

"Ye' are Iain MacIntosh. I'm no' mistaken in that, am I?" she asked again.

"I was," he answered at last. "But that was a very long time ago. I'm called only by my number here. Fifty-One."

It was the number taken from the order in which the ghosts had risen after their deaths. He'd been the fifty-first. Why or what determined that order, he had no idea. He knew only that after two centuries, he'd almost forgotten Iain and begun to think of himself simply as Fifty-One.

He didn't even know why he was numbered among these men. Perhaps it was his hatred, like theirs, that had kept him chained to this place for so many years. Perhaps all he needed in order to move on was revenge against the man who had caused his death. His and all the others.

Either that, or he simply needed to let go of the anger that bound him to this place.

But that wasn't going to happen. The man who had been the cause of their ruin had himself lived a long life, with benefit of hearth and home, while Iain and the others who'd lost their lives at Culloden had moldered in mass graves, tossed one on top of the other like rotted scraps.

If giving up his hatred was the only way to move on, Iain was cursed to eternity in this place.

"Or perhaps you could earn yer chance at taking yer revenge on yer Prince, just as I offered, aye?" Soni asked, her expression far too innocent. "One wee task to prove yer worthiness is all it will take to cut the ties that bind ye' to Culloden Moor. Are ye' ready?"

"It's my turn, then, is it?"

He'd waited for this moment from the first, hanging back, fearing she'd set her eyes upon him next. Fearing she wouldn't.

"Aye, yer time has come, Fifty-One. Time for ye' to earn yer way to what ye' desire most. If yer willing to sacrifice for it, that is. If yer willing to give up all that ye've held dear."

A mist swirled around them as she spoke, a haze of green that blocked all the others from his sight, as if he and Soni were locked away from the rest of the world in their own private chamber.

Iain nodded, straightening to his full height. "What would you have of me, lass?"

Whatever it was she asked, he would give the task his all. He would do anything for his own opportunity to show the faithless prince what his careless actions had caused. Anything for his own opportunity to purge the rage that had grown in his heart for well over two hundred years. Anything to free his soul from the unending nothingness of Culloden Moor.

"An act of heroism. A selfless act, to save the life of an innocent. Are ye' prepared for whatever ye' might face in this task, and willing to pay the price after you've completed it?"

"I am." He paused for a moment, staring into the girl's unfathomable eyes. "As long as I have the opportunity for my revenge when the task is done."

"Oh, you'll have that opportunity, Fifty-One. Once you've earned it. If you still want it once you've completed yer task, that is. If ye've no' changed yer mind by that time."

Changed his mind?

He choked back a bitter cough of laughter. Of course he would want it. It was his one desire to break the curse that bound him to this mournful plain. No task he could imagine, no matter how burdensome or difficult, would ever change his mind.

"Indeed," Soni murmured, a smile lighting her eyes before it touched her lips. "We shall see, Iain MacIntosh. We shall see."

The swirling mist grew in its intensity, a vortex of wind and color that seemed to press in on him from every direction. The pressure grew, pounding against his ears, filling his lungs with an unfamiliar breath of air, bringing with it an awareness of his body that he hadn't felt for centuries. He could feel his feet lifting off the ground, his body whirling faster and faster as the mist turned from green to black.

Not yet! He had questions that needed answering before she sent him on.

"How will I ken when I've done what I need to do? How will I ken who it is I'm to help? When—"

Soni's laughter tinkled over the sound of the rushing wind that filled his ears and choked off his words.

"All in good time, Fifty-One. You'll ken everything, all in good time. Until we meet again."

CHAPTER TWO

Toliver Mine
Colorado
Present Day

"Don't be ridiculous, Dale. You're not in love with me. You don't even know me."

Salome Addison pushed away from the man attempting to pull her into his arms, and tried to ignore the odd emotion flashing in his eyes. She continued to back away, skirting the stacks of supplies in the small room. With the boxes in between her and Dale, she stopped, as if the barrier gave her enough protection to confront the situation.

"I can't believe you don't feel the same way I do, Sallie." Dale took a step toward her but stopped when she held up her hand. "Okay, okay. I get that you're not totally won over yet. But you will be. I love you and you love me, whether you're ready to admit it or not. I've known the truth of that from the moment I first saw you. Anyone with half a brain can see we're meant to be together."

"Love?" she managed to squeak, though her throat tightened on the word. "You've only known me for two weeks."

Love didn't happen in two weeks. It didn't even happen in two months. Though she might have believed in such a silly thing in her past, Sallie had grown beyond such foolishness, though the lessons hadn't been easy. She had enough failed romances in her past to be the walking poster child for proof that love at first sight didn't exist.

There had been Roy, the classic biker/bad boy who had swept her off her feet when she'd met him at the cafe where she'd been waitressing during her time in college. That had lasted until she'd learned that he was really a dentist trying to "find himself." He'd bought a bike, invented a persona, and taken a holiday from his real job. Unfortunately, he'd also "taken a holiday" from his real wife.

Roy was followed by Colin, a pre-med student who swore he was in love and ready to settle down. It only took three months to learn that what he was really looking for was a sugar mama to do his wash and fix his meals so he could concentrate on his studies. Except he didn't concentrate on his studies as much as he concentrated on all the other women who were more than willing to be his sugar mamas, too.

Most recently there had been Clint, a rodeo cowboy who had at first seemed the perfect fit. He said he came from a ranching family just like she did and wanted nothing more than to settle down on a piece of land where he could raise cows and a family. Sallie had thought for sure he was the one until she learned that the closest he'd ever been to a bull was the mechanical version in the western bar where he liked to spend his nights. And as far as the riding he did, well, it wasn't horses that drew his attention. It was all those girls who were looking for a special night or two with what they also thought was a real cowboy.

No, love at first sight didn't exist. Especially not for someone like her with a history of always choosing the wrong guy. At least she had learned a thing or two from her history of poor dating choices. She'd learned enough to know right now that the man on the other side of these boxes was definitely another one of those wrong guys, no matter how handsome he might be.

"Two weeks or two years, makes no difference," Dale said confidently, giving her a wink. "You might as well accept it, Sallie. It's going to be you and me in the end. I know it as sure as I'm standing here."

Sallie struggled with how to respond to something so obviously outside the boundaries of normal. Even if he was as naive as she'd once been, his actions weren't those of a rational person.

"Listen, Dale, I don't know what you think you feel for me, but there is nothing between us and there's not going to be anything. I don't mix romance and work. This job means too much to me to risk it on some summer fling."

After four years at the Toliver Mine, Sallie finally felt as though she'd found someplace where she could be happy. She might have made mistakes in her past, but those days were behind her. It took her a long time to grow up, but she'd finally rounded that corner. No man was going to pull the rug out from under her ever again.

And if she wasn't going to let a man mess up her life, she sure wasn't going to mess it up herself.

"We're not a summer fling, darlin'," he said, starting toward her. "We're a for-keeps kind of thing, so you might as well start getting used to the idea."

The flirty smile he'd worn moments before morphed into something else. Something that made Sallie distinctly uncomfortable.

Fortunately, the echoing of the old train whistle heading into the stop up the hill distracted him and she was able to make her escape through the door and out into the warm sun. Her steps quickened until she was moving at a steady jog, heading toward the train station where her co-workers would be gathered.

After the experience she'd just had with Dale, she wanted all the company she could get. Whether the guy simply had a sick sense of humor or he was seriously off his meds didn't matter. Behavior like his wouldn't be tolerated in this environment. Besides, seriously? Love at first sight? Did he really expect her or any other woman to fall for that? Couldn't happen. Didn't exist. Especially not with someone who was so determined to make it happen, no matter that the object of his affection had no interest in him, whatsoever. It took more than eyes meeting across a crowded room to connect with the man of your dreams. Thank heaven she'd finally learned that lesson.

Switching gears from jog to run, she made a quick mental note to give the other girls working at the mine a heads-up about Dale's odd behavior. No point in their being as unpleasantly surprised as she had been.

She skidded to a stop in the loose gravel at the base of the stairs to the train platform, breathless from her uphill run. Halfway up the stairs, an excited bubble of chatter hit her ears.

From the sound of the conversation, the new guy had finally arrived.

Another ten steps up to the platform and she was forced to slightly revise her earlier conclusion. Love at first sight might not exist, but attraction at first sight definitely did.

* * *

A jostle awakened Iain, bumping his head against a pane of glass. It wasn't seriously painful, but it was hard enough to jolt him awake.

He was on a conveyance of some sort, that much was clear. A train, he'd guess, based on the books he'd seen in the visitors' center at Culloden. It had been his impression that these beasts weren't much in use anymore. Not since automobiles had become so popular. Perhaps he'd been mistaken.

His head still rested against the glass as the train rounded a sharp curve, the momentum jerking his body once again. This time the bump was much harder, rapping his forehead against the glass. Only as he lifted his fingers to touch the warm skin did the magnitude of what had just happened settle over him.

His contact with the glass had hurt. He could feel the pain. Feel the warmth of his own skin under his fingers just as he had when he was alive.

It would seem there was much the little Muir witch had neglected to tell him.

11

One long shriek of the whistle sounded and the train began to slow. Iain sat up straight and braced himself this time, not willing to experiment with another crack of his head against the glass. He scanned the car around him, noting that he was the only passenger.

When the train jerked to a full stop, he stood and slowly made his way to the end of the car and out the opening.

About ten feet away, several identically-clad men had gathered, all smiling expectantly, as if they had known he'd be getting off the train.

Another tidbit of information Soni had neglected to share?

"Welcome!" the closest of the group called as he approached, hand extended in greeting. "We'd begun to worry that you weren't going to get here before opening day."

"I'm here now," Iain said, unsure of what his response should be since he had no idea where *here* actually was.

"So you are. And with plenty of time to get you trained, too. I'm Justin, by the way. Justin Heath. Over there is Dusty Kramer and Tony Juarez." Each of the men lifted a hand in acknowledgment as Justin said their names. "And coming up the stairs we have Manda Turner and Ashley Billings. I'm afraid Ms. Toliver didn't leave us your name. She only said that she'd arranged for another employee who would be showing up before we opened for the summer."

Iain dipped his head respectfully as he was introduced, his mind scrambling to keep up with his new situation. They thought he was supposed to be here. They thought he was the worker they had been expecting. Since Soni had sent him here, maybe he was.

"I'm called Iain," he said, finding it easier than he had expected to slip into his old self again. "Iain MacIntosh."

"Oh, my Lord," one of the women said, rolling her eyes. "Did you hear that luscious accent? We're going to have all the women from nine to ninety swooning on the mountain this summer, sure enough. Probably end up doubling our repeat business."

"No kidding, Manda," the other woman said with a chuckle. "And they'll all want to be on his tour, just so they can listen to him talk. Better get him trained fast, Justin. He's going to be one busy little bee."

"The ladies are probably right," Justin agreed with a grin. "Though we'll need to get you out of that kilt thing you're wearing and into standard issue. And, right on cue, here's just the woman to take care of those little details."

Iain turned his gaze toward the woman stepping up on the platform and, for just an instant, he felt as if his newly-beating heart had ceased to function all over again.

Her eyes were a brown so rich, they reminded him of freshly tilled soil in the early spring. And the rest of her was nothing to scoff at, either. He couldn't bring himself to tear his gaze from her when Justin spoke again.

"This is our senior guide, Sallie Addison. Nancy, Ms. Toliver that is, probably told you that Sallie is the one she put in charge up here. She'll be the one training you, too, since she's been here longer than almost any of us. Isn't that right, Sallie?"

Sallie moved closer, her eyes locked on Iain's. Several long seconds passed before she spoke, almost as if the two of them existed in those seconds outside time.

"Yes," she said at last. "That will be me. Come on, Iain, let's give you a tour and get you into the right clothes."

"Or, better yet, out of them," Manda said as they passed by her and a giggling Ashley.

At the bottom of the stairs Sallie stopped and turned to face him, her cheeks and neck colored with a healthy blush.

"I'm sorry about that," she said, her eyes darting back up to the platform they'd just left. "I'll have a chat with Manda later. We do a lot of joking around up here, but I don't want you starting off your summer with us feeling harassed."

"Yer under the impression the lady's words upset me?" he asked, hoping she'd look up at him again rather than continuing to study the tip of her shoe. "I'm no' possessed of such a delicate nature, Mistress Addison. Of that, you can rest assured."

He touched a hand to her shoulder and her blush deepened by several shades.

"Well...okay. Good. Okay, then," she mumbled. "And it's just Sallie. There are no formalities here at the mine."

He could almost swear she trembled beneath his touch. As for his physical response to her, well, he could only suppose it must be the result of his having been, literally, out of touch with women for the past two hundred seventy years.

"Okay," she said again, this time moving away a couple of steps before turning her back on him. "You've met everyone but Dale. There are only eight of us for the summer, but it will feel like more than that once the tourists start arriving. The barracks are over this direction.

I'll show you where you can put your things and then we'll get your shirts and shorts."

Shorts. That must be what they called those wee trousers they all wore. Exactly the same material for both the men and the women, though the design was different. The men's were baggy and hit below their knees while the women's were much shorter and more fitted. So fitted, in fact, there could definitely be no mistaking which of their number were females. Like the one walking ahead of him now.

No mistaking at all.

"This is the mine entrance," Sallie said, drawing his attention from her backside. "This open area is where we gather all the tourists when they come down from the train. Our camp is just ahead, farther down into the clearing."

After a few more minutes of walking down the steep hillside, they reached several buildings in a small valley, continuing on until they reached the door of the longest building.

"This is the men's quarters," she said, knocking and then pausing a moment before she opened the door for him to enter. "Mind your step going in. The rains have washed away a little gully here. Showers and toilets are through that door at the end of the room."

The room itself was fairly spartan, holding only six identical beds with a tall cabinet separating each bed from the other. Sallie led him to the closest bed and opened the door of the cabinet next to it to reveal a large empty space with drawers below.

"This is your bed and you can keep your things in here." Her voice faltered for a moment as she glanced down at his hands and back up. "Though, I can't help but notice you don't appear to have brought anything with you."

"Lost in transit," he said, smiling what he hoped was an apologetic smile. "I've only what you see before you and nothing else."

He hadn't really had much of a need for luggage and spare clothing where he'd been.

She nodded thoughtfully, her teeth worrying at her bottom lip for a moment. "In that case, I guess we'd better issue you a few sets of clothing. I have a spare toothbrush and some toiletries I can let you have until one of us makes a trip into town."

"That would be most welcome," he answered, stepping outside again as she pushed open the door for him.

He turned as she followed, just in time to catch her as her foot slid into the washed-out depression in front of the door, pitching her forward. Her head fit against his chest as her fingers grasped his arms. Without thought, he pulled her close, and her body molded against his. Bending his head forward, his chin rested against her hair and the scent of fresh flowers filled his nostrils.

"Sorry," she mumbled into his chest.

He wasn't. Not in the least. For a fact, he couldn't imagine one single thing he would rather do than stand here in the warmth of the sun with Sallie Addison in his arms. Well, nothing he'd rather do out here in the open.

"Are you unharmed, my lady?"

"What?" she asked, her face turning up toward him.

Those eyes! And lips so plump and pink it was as if they dared him to take a taste.

"I'm…no, I'm…fine," she stammered. "Nothing's damaged except my pride."

"If you'll but direct me to where you store yer tools, I'll see to it that hole is set to rights," he offered, still holding her in his arms.

She nodded, also making no effort to move away.

"What's going on here?" A man, one who hadn't been on the platform earlier, stood only a few feet away, his hands on his hips. "Who are you?"

Sallie stiffened in Iain's arms, her head snapping around toward the newcomer.

"This is Iain MacIntosh, Dale. He's the new guy we've been expecting," she said, at last pushing away to stand on her own. "I tripped coming out of the barracks and his quick reaction saved me from a nasty fall."

"That's awfully convenient," Dale said, his face a dark cloud of emotion.

"No, what would have been convenient would have been if you would have filled in this hole yesterday when I heard Justin ask you to do exactly that."

"Justin's not my boss," Dale grumbled, crossing his arms in front of him. "He could have done it just as easily as asking me to do it."

"Whatever," Sallie sighed, turning back toward Iain. "This is Dale Nichols. He's the only one of us you didn't meet up at the train. Now that you've met everyone, we can continue on. Let's get those clothes for you. Once you get changed, we can finish the tour."

She walked ahead of him as before, pulling keys out of her pocket as they approached a small building set closer to the hillside. Much to Iain's displeasure, Dale fell into step beside him.

"This is our storage for all sorts of things," Sallie said as she unlocked the door and stepped inside.

"So you're the new guy," Dale said, his arms crossed in front of him. "What took you so long to get here?"

Iain shrugged. "It was a long journey to get to this place."

"You from Scotland?" Dale asked. "Doesn't make sense to me. I can't imagine why Ms. Toliver would need to hire a foreigner. There are plenty of guys she could have hired from around here."

"No, there aren't," Sallie said as she rejoined them, her arms filled with plaid flannel and khaki. "We had the job posted for months without one single applicant. Here you go, Iain. If I have the size wrong, we can switch them out. You get changed into these and meet me at the gathering spot in front of the mine that I pointed out to you. I'll show you where you'll be working for the summer. As for you, Dale, I recommend you go get a shovel and do what Justin asked."

Inside the barracks, Iain changed into a pair of the shorts and one of the shirts. Once he was done, he folded the clothing he had taken off. The last time he could remember putting these things on was the day he'd died in them. The memory shuddered through his body and he couldn't help but run his hand over his old shirt one more time, surprised not to find bullet holes in the cloth.

Apparently, there was nothing too difficult for the witch who'd sent him to this place.

"There's something I think you need to know." Dale stood inside the doorway, a shovel in his hands.

"And that is?" Iain asked, beginning to think he just might dislike this man.

"Don't you go getting any ideas about Sallie. She belongs to me, so you can just keep your hands, and your eyes, off her. Yeah, I saw how you were looking at her."

"Yer her husband?" Iain asked, no longer unsure about his dislike of the man.

"No. Not yet," Dale answered, his eyes darting around the room.

"Then banns have been read for yer betrothal?" Iain clarified. "You've set a date?"

"No," Dale said again. "But it's only a matter of time. Sallie is mine, so you just keep your distance, Scotchman, you hear? Don't you forget my warning. It's the last one you get."

Iain didn't plan to forget anything about this conversation. Nothing that twisted at a man's guts the way Dale's words twisted at his was easily forgotten. It was as if someone had laid claim to something that belonged to him, and then dared him to do anything about it. Iain couldn't begin to explain why he felt the way he did. He only knew that he did. Perhaps it was no more than some strange result of his being alive again after having felt nothing at all for so very long.

He shook his head as he closed the door to the cabinet, trying to rid himself of these strange emotions. He wasn't here to challenge Dale for the woman. A woman like her would have to belong to someone. He was here to save a life so that he could get on with the next step in his own journey, confronting the man who was responsible for his death.

None of these trivial social interactions mattered. Not his feelings, not Dale, and not Sallie. Especially not Sallie.

Though, even as Iain thought the words, he already knew it was going to take some effort to convince himself he really meant them.

CHAPTER THREE

"What would Nancy do?"

Sallie said the words aloud in an attempt to reinforce her determination to be the manager Nancy Toliver expected her to be. Dale's odd behavior was hard enough to accept, all by itself. If he was going to spend the summer shirking the extra work assigned to him, there was no doubt about what she needed to do. At some point, she was going to have to stiffen her backbone and lay down the law, just like Nancy would have done if she were here.

A smile tickled around the corners of her mouth in spite of her worries as she considered how many more clichés she could come up with before she actually made herself do what needed doing. Nancy had trusted Sallie enough to put her in charge. The old lady had trusted her enough to leave her home, her animals, and the running of the mine tours in her hands. There was no way Sallie was going to let her employer, her friend, down. If that meant getting tough, then she'd walk the walk.

"There's another one," she whispered, clutching her clipboard to her chest, fighting the urge to laugh out loud.

Maybe that meant she was one phrase closer to being the quality manager Nancy deserved.

Turning her gaze back toward the camp, Sallie spotted Iain striding her direction. She could only hope this one would be a strong enough team member to make up for Dale's shortfalls. There had to be some reason Nancy had chosen him, other than his exceedingly good looks.

He waved as he approached and for just a second or two, she suspected that his looks might have had more to do with Nancy's choice than she was giving the old woman credit for. As Nancy herself was fond of saying, she might be too old to play, but she still enjoyed looking.

"I see they fit," Sallie said as Iain joined her, embarrassed the moment the words popped out of her mouth.

Boy, did they ever fit. As good as he'd looked in the kilt, he looked equally good now.

"Aye," he agreed with a grin that sent a shiver up her spine. "You've a good eye for judging a man."

It was all she could do not to laugh out loud at his comment. If only he knew just what a lousy judge of men she'd always been. But lousy history or not, she could already tell she'd need to be careful with this one. Her best defense was to keep the relationship purely business.

"Okay, then," she said, as much to focus herself as for his benefit. "As I told you before, this is the gathering spot for all our visitors. You can see we're not far from the river. One of our challenges every year is to keep our guests away from the banks. Considering the heavy rains we're having and the melt upstream, that's even more important this year than it usually is. Someone falls in there, chances are close to one-hundred percent they're not coming out alive."

Iain nodded, his eyes fixed on the raging waters tearing down the mountain. "Could you no' build a fence of some sort to call attention to the drop?"

"As a matter of fact, we had one until last week. The floods coming down ate the bank right out from under the metal poles. If we walk over this way a little, you can see them sticking out of the muddy water." She led him closer to the river, stopping before they got anywhere near the edge. "Even when we had the fence, we still had to do the warnings. Kids always seemed to think the fence was for climbing on rather than for stopping them. Down that way, toward our camp, is the turnoff that leads to the petting zoo. I'll show you that later. And back up that way, toward the train stop, is the turnoff that goes to the picnic and gold panning areas."

"Gold panning?" Iain echoed, his brow wrinkling as he glanced over his shoulder toward the gaping mouth of the Toliver Mine.

"The tourists love it," Sallie said, leading him away from the water and back toward the mine entrance. "There's only trace amounts of gold washing down the river, but people enjoy trying their hand at it. It's a big Friday evening draw for families, along with the cookouts. All in all, we do a lot more here to entertain our guests than just tour through the mine."

Though, hands down, the mine was still the biggest attraction. She stopped at the entrance and lifted the lid on a big plastic box, pulling out two hard hats and handing one to Iain.

"Everyone who goes past this opening wears one of these. Safety regulation number one," she said with a grin. "I should have asked if you'd like a jacket. It's always much cooler in the mine."

"Cold is no bother to me," he said, an odd expression flickering in his eyes.

"In that case, follow me, but watch your step. The tracks for the rail carts make for some tricky footwork in a couple of places. And just to make it harder, there are puddles everywhere, so if you step off the boards we have in place, you're going to end up with wet feet."

For the next half hour, she led him through the mine, just as if he were one of her tour groups. Going through her regular spiel, she relaxed, slipping into her comfort zone here on familiar turf. Nothing in the mine could put her off her game.

Nothing until the lights went out, that is.

It was a regular part of the tour. Something that made the kids squeal and more than a few of the adults suck in their breath. It was a moment designed to allow everyone to experience the mine as it had been in the beginning, bereft of any man-made light. A flip of the switch and the cavern went dark. A pause to let her audience understand the true meaning of being in a cave and then she'd strike a match to light one of the original lanterns the miners had used.

Only this time, for some reason she couldn't begin to explain, once the lights went out, things felt very different. No little kids screaming. No nervous giggles or feet shuffling. Just a profound silence, punctuated by the soft sounds of two people breathing. And, louder than

24

anything else, her own heartbeat, pounding in her chest, faster and louder with each passing second.

She could only pray that it was the blood in her ears she heard, a sound that would, hopefully, allude her companion.

When she struck the match, she wasn't at all surprised to find her hand shaking, considering the last few seconds. For the first time ever, the match went out as she tried to light the lantern, almost as if some mysterious breeze had fluttered by and puffed upon the flame.

"Allow me," Iain said, his hands covering hers to take the matches from her grasp.

She could swear that she felt his presence around her, like a warm cloak floating down to land on her shoulders. An instant later the match flared to life, a bright flash harsh against her eyes after the intense black. Another second and the lantern flared to life.

Iain stood so close she could feel the heat wafting from his body. Only with the greatest determination was she able to keep herself from leaning into him.

"Yer shivering," he said. "Perhaps yer advice for a jacket would have been well taken, aye?"

"I'm fine," she muttered, flipping the switch to turn the electricity back on before turning to retrace their steps to the entrance. "We'll have you tag along on a couple of real tours. Then you'll lead a couple and I'll tag along to make sure you're comfortable with it. Does that sound like—"

As she spoke, she suddenly realized Iain was no longer at her side.

"Iain? Iain!"

"I'm just here," he called, his voice echoing from a dark tunnel off the main path.

When she hurried in his direction, she could see the lantern he still carried, a small light bobbing in the distance.

"Stop right there!" she yelled at him. "Not another step!"

"This is no' the way?"

"No, sir, it is not," she answered, grabbing his arm as she reached his side. "This area is dangerous. There's a pit just a little farther down this way that's been the end of more than one miner. Come on. No one should be down here."

She slid her hand down his arm to tangle her fingers with his, pulling him away from the detour.

"No lights," Iain murmured. "I should have guessed I was headed the wrong way."

"Not your fault," Sallie consoled. "Accident averted. I'll need to get Justin down here to fix that before someone else wanders off the rails."

At the bend in the tunnel where Iain had taken his wrong turn, Sallie stopped, staring back down into the dark. "I could have sworn the caution tape was across this opening when we came by this way."

But, obviously, she had been wrong. Just went to show how her mind could make her think something was where it belonged because she expected it to be there. It wasn't just that the warning tape had come loose and fallen to the ground. There was none of the yellow tape anywhere around. A mystery that needed solving, to be sure. But the mystery wasn't near as high on the list of priorities as getting a new barrier erected.

* * *

"Who is Salome?" Iain asked.

"What did you say?" Sallie asked, stopping mid-stride and turning back to face him. "Where did you hear that name?"

Though Sallie clearly doubted herself about the warning in the mine, she had been correct. There had been a barrier of yellow ribbons strung across the opening to the secondary tunnel when they'd passed that opening. Iain remembered having seen it because, at the time, he'd wondered about it, but hadn't wanted to interrupt her story about the original miners to ask. The fact that the barrier wasn't there now was only confirmation of what Iain had suspected while they were inside. Someone else had been in the mine with them. Someone who had followed them while Sallie had gone through his training. Someone who had spied upon them. And, more to the point, someone who had hidden in the side tunnel when they were on their way out.

That same someone had made just enough noise to attract their attention. Someone who had whispered the name *Salome*. Without a doubt, the someone in question had done his best to get them to follow him down the dangerous side tunnel.

Iain shook his head, staring back in the direction of the tunnel they'd been down, wishing he'd had more opportunity to investigate who might still be hiding there.

"In the tunnel," he answered at last. "I thought I heard someone calling out for Salome."

Sallie's eyes went wide for a moment and she crossed her arms protectively in front of her, hands rubbing against her skin like someone trying to ward off a chill.

"I don't see how that's possible," she said. "No one was in there but you and me. Not unless you believe in ghosts."

The chuckle she ended on sounded half-hearted to him.

"I've no call to doubt their existence," he said. Especially not since he was one. "Is Salome a ghost?"

"No," Sallie answered, starting forward again, her steps a little quicker than they had been before. "I'm Salome. It's my real name, though I'm not at all fond of it. I much prefer Sallie."

Just like that, as surely as if he'd been given the name of the person he was supposed to protect, Iain knew that Sallie was the one he'd been sent here to save. Why the man she was promised to wasn't the one responsible for saving her, he couldn't imagine. All he knew was that it had to be her. He'd never before in the whole of his life met anyone who he had instantly felt such a great need to protect.

He glanced over at her as they walked toward the camp. She wore her long, brown hair gathered up with a band at the back of her head. It cascaded down to the middle of her back, swinging hypnotically from side to side with each step she took.

He was mesmerized by her every movement, her every word. Her voice held a melodic note when she spoke that reminded him of his old granny's stories about the wild Faeries who lived in the woods near his childhood home.

Yes, without a doubt, Sallie was the reason he was here. She was the innocent he'd been sent to save. Knowing that left him only one task. The task of discovering what—or who—he was meant to save her from.

And though he'd never been a man drawn to gambling, Iain was willing to bet his life that the *who* he needed to save her from was the same person who'd followed them inside Toliver Mine. The same person who'd called her name from the depths of that shaft.

CHAPTER FOUR

Some people were simply born to be cooks. Creating wonderful food was a gift, a talent, just like painting or singing or sculpting.

In Sallie's opinion, Manda Turner was one of those gifted people. Since Manda had joined their crew, the smells wafting through the camp were equaled only by the meals themselves.

Tonight was no exception.

While the dinner itself had been delicious, it was the dessert Sallie had been waiting for since the first hints of cinnamon and apples had tickled her senses.

The crew had drifted into the dining hall in ones and twos as they finished their chores until, at last, almost everyone was present. Justin appeared to have taken the new guy, Iain, under his wing, including him at the table where he always ate with Dusty and Tony. It had been this way since the first day Iain had arrived.

A sense of well-being settled over Sallie as she dipped her spoon into the steaming mound of apple goodness. They had a good group of guides this year. Justin had started the same year she had and the others, except for

Iain and Dale, had come the year after. The personalities meshed well, as evidenced by the volume of the conversation, interrupted frequently by comfortable laughter.

It was shaping up to be a good year at the Toliver, though tomorrow would be the true test. Tomorrow was the first day the tours would open for the season and, from the last tally she'd seen, every tour was booked full.

Sallie's first bite had finally cooled enough for her to pop it into her mouth. She closed her eyes, allowing her senses to revel in the flavors playing over her tongue.

This was life as it should be, an excellent ending to a great day. The beginning of a great season. Nothing could steal from her the lovely calm that settled on her shoulders.

"Here's my woman," Dale said, dropping his tray down beside hers. "The day has dragged while I waited to see you again."

Maybe there was something that could steal her calm, after all.

Sallie opened her eyes as Dale fit himself into the seat next to her. When he scooted his chair closer and nudged his foot next to hers, the dessert in front of her lost its appeal.

Just as well. Those were surely calories she didn't need. Besides, she still had chores of her own to do.

As she pushed her chair back to stand, Dale's hand shot out to grab her wrist.

"Where do you think you're going? I just got here."

"Then I guess you'll have to move over to one of the other tables if you want company while you eat," she said, forcing a smile to her lips. "I have animals waiting for me to get them their dinner."

Thank goodness. The company of the petting zoo inhabitants was highly preferable to that of her current companion.

A quick twist of her hand and she was free of Dale's touch. Free to escape into the approaching twilight of a Colorado mountain evening.

The sheep and goats bleated their welcome as she approached, sending a twinge of guilt through her chest. She should have done this before she'd gone in to feed herself. Even the pigs looked happy to see her. Only the old llama, as usual, remained indifferent to her arrival.

She'd have to bring them all a special treat tomorrow to make amends. Maybe Manda would have some leftover apples.

Barely five minutes into hauling feed from the shed, a noise from somewhere in the direction of the trees set her nerves twitching. When a gentle hand touched her shoulder, she jumped and dropped the bucket she held.

"For crying out loud," she said once she realized it was Iain who stood beside her. "You scared me half to death. Don't you know any better than to creep up on people like that?"

The grin on his face did little to calm her pounding heart.

"My apologies, Sallie," he said, before bending down to retrieve her bucket. "I'd no intention to frighten you. I've seen you out here each night and on this night I thought to offer my assistance with the feeding."

Her first instinct was to reject his offer. Time spent with the animals was one of her favorite tasks and she had no real desire to hasten it along. On the other hand, watering them meant using the old pump and having a strong arm to help with that particular part of the process would be a welcome change.

"I suppose you can help, if you really want to," she said, realizing as she spoke she sounded less than inviting. "But you need to make sure you aren't going to get all freaked out when they come at you. Some of them are older and they need a calm hand."

"You've no call to worry yerself over that," Iain said, his grin giving way to a serious expression. "I grew up around beasts such as these. They'll no' rattle my composure. If anything, they'll calm me as much as I calm them. It's been a number of years since I've had the pleasure of interacting with their like."

"Really? I was raised around animals, too. On my family's ranch out in the eastern part of the state. To be honest, being able to work with these guys was the one thing that originally drew me to this job. Though, now, of course, I love everything about what I do here at Toliver Mine."

Why couldn't she just shut up and enjoy the moment? If they gave awards for diarrhea of the mouth, she should be at the head of the line for winning that one. For some reason, being around Iain made her nervous and when she got nervous, she couldn't quit talking. It had happened every single day as she'd gone through his training. She could only wonder at what he thought of her.

No, strike that. She'd been such a doofus around him, she really didn't want to know what he thought of her.

With an effort, she clamped her lips together, putting her full concentration into the old pump handle.

"Here," Iain said, his voice a warm blanket of rolling brogue as he gently pushed her to one side. "Let me do that. You switch the buckets."

He assumed her spot at the pump, appearing to easily do with one arm that which had taken her whole body strength to accomplish.

"I've a curiosity," he said as they carried their filled buckets back to the pens. "I hope you'll no' take offense if I ask something personal. It's been on my mind since the day I first arrived."

"Ask away," she said, hurrying to keep up with the speed at which he pumped taking the better part of her concentration. "I promise not to be offended."

"Why is it that Dale is no' out here helping you with yer evening chores?"

The muscles in his arms flexed and contracted with each pump of the handle, distracting her almost to the point of preventing her from answering.

"I don't…" She swallowed and pulled her gaze from his arm before trying again. "That's an odd question. Why would you expect Dale to be out here helping me?"

A puzzled expression wrinkled Iain's brow. "I should think it obvious. He told me yer to be wed, the two of you. That being the case, I canna ken why he'd leave you to do this work on yer own."

"What?" Sallie jerked upright so quickly that water in the bucket she held sloshed out onto her bare legs. "He actually said those words to you? That's so not true. I have absolutely no relationship whatsoever with Dale. I've only known him for a few weeks. People don't fall in love in just a couple of weeks and they sure as heck don't plan to get married in that length of time."

Sallie had harbored the hope that Dale had given up all the nonsense about their being meant to be together. Apparently he hadn't.

"It could happen," Iain said quietly, continuing to work the pump handle up and down. "My own grandmother swore that an ancestor of hers had worked in a castle where everyone had been touched by a Faerie's blessing, decreeing that they and all their families should find their own true loves. When those people were brought together, falling in love was no' a matter of time. It happened in the first moments they laid eyes upon one another." He stopped pumping and straightened up, a smile playing around the corners of his lips. "Or so my grandmother claimed."

Was this guy for real?

"Yeah, well, in spite of what your grandmother told you, I'm not a big believer in Faeries," Sallie said. "So, in my Faerie-less world, people don't fall in love and decide to get married instantly. And even if they did, I can assure you, Dale is not my true love. If I feel anything for him at all, it's major irritation that he's acting this way. To be honest, he's beginning to make me really uncomfortable."

And more than a little angry.

Iain nodded, the smile disappearing as his eyes clouded before he looked away. He picked up the two filled buckets at his feet and waited while Sallie started forward. In silence, they began to fill the troughs in each of the animal pens. They'd emptied all the buckets before he spoke again.

"I've considered yer situation, and, as I see it, yer best plan would be to have yer men folk speak with Dale."

"My men folk?" Sallie chuckled, wiping her damp hands on the legs of her shorts. "I'm not sure who you mean when you suggest that, but I can assure you, I'm the one who'll be having a chat with Dale."

Iain stopped, his expression more serious than she'd seen before. "His behavior is unseemly. It's the men of yer family who should speak to him on yer behalf. Have you no father, no brothers to look after yer interests in the world?"

What a quaint, old-fashioned response. Quaint, old-fashioned and more than a little sexist. Sallie studied her companion a moment before answering, deciding at last that he meant no disrespect by his comments. Maybe such views were openly held wherever he'd been raised. Whatever his reasoning, she would do her best to take his comments in the spirit in which they'd been offered.

"I don't have any brothers, Iain. And my dad lives too far away for me to expect him to fight my battles for me." She gave him what she hoped was a reassuring smile. "I've learned to do that for myself. There's no need to worry about it. I can take care of myself."

Besides, her father had made it pretty clear that she was on her own after her last bad relationship.

Iain held her gaze for a moment, then shifted his focus to the persistent sheep butting against his leg. With a thoughtful smile, he reached down to scratch the animal's head. The sheep's contented bleating drowned out his response, but she could have sworn he mumbled something about this being the reason he was here.

* * *

"What did you say?"

Iain looked up from the attention-hog at his feet to find Sallie staring at him, her eyes round with disbelief. Careless of him to have spoken his thoughts aloud.

"Only that I've missed this since I've been here," he lied, dipping his head to indicate the animal he stroked. "There's never any question of where you stand with beasts of the field. They either like you or no' leaving little enough room to wonder or worry."

He knew his answer had satisfied her when she sighed and let out her breath in a chuckle, a soft smile relaxing the lines on her lovely face.

"True enough," she agreed. "I've often thought that I prefer their company to that of people."

There was a sentiment he could accept. He'd felt that way often enough himself.

"When I was younger, this was how I dreamed of spending my life. A small plot of land, animals to tend, a woman of my own, a family to greet me each night. There was life to strive toward."

Why he shared something so intimate, he had no idea. He could only be thankful that he'd stopped himself before he'd said more. Before he'd said what was really on his mind. Before he'd said that what he'd dreamed of was a woman like the one who shared this moment with him now.

"Simple enough dreams," Sallie said with a smile. "And yet, you left your home and traveled thousands of miles to come here. Why? What brought you here?"

"A quest of sorts," he answered, unwilling to tell her more. "A settling of one part of my existence so that I might get on with the next."

She nodded as if trying to understand his cryptic response. As gentle and kind as this woman seemed, he doubted she'd be impressed with a man who needed his full measure of revenge in order to pass into the beyond. When he tried to see himself through her eyes, he wasn't sure that he was all that impressed, either.

He helped as she gathered buckets and they carried everything back to the small shed at the corner of the pens.

A glance over to her confirmed what he already knew. He should have come out to help her the first night he'd seen her out here. Instead, he'd allowed himself to be swayed by Dale's claim of possession. Knowing the truth had brought him an odd sense of relief that clung to him now, wrapping him in a fuzzy warm cocoon of strange emotions.

At least now he understood better why he'd been sent to help her. She had no men folk of her own to be there for her.

"No, let me," he said, jumping in front of her to grab the grain sack she reached for.

"If you want to," she said with a grin as she backed away. "But I lift these things all the time. I'm not some delicate little...hey, you okay?"

"Yes," he lied.

In truth, the pain that shot through his hand when he reached under the grain sack was next to intolerable. He straightened and lifted the sack away to find a coiled snake. A snake, which from the feel of it, had just bitten him.

"Holy crapola!" Sallie squealed, taking a step back. "Get away from that thing, Iain. That's a rattler, sure as

I'm standing here. It didn't bite you, did it? They're poisonous."

"No, it didn't," he said, dropping the sack at his feet to stare at his hand.

Two distinct holes adorned the back of his hand, slowly closing, disappearing as he watched. So, he could feel pain, but suffered no ill effects. Maybe he wasn't quite as alive as he'd thought himself to be. Perhaps there was an advantage to being a ghost.

"Are you sure? Let me see," Sallie ordered, pulling his hand into hers to examine it. "Okay, I guess you're right. I thought for sure the way you'd jerked back...but I guess not. Thank goodness. That could have gone so badly."

It certainly could have. If Sallie had been the one to pick up that bag as she did every night.

He allowed her to hold his hand, turning it back and forth as if she couldn't believe his good luck. He should have pulled away from her much sooner than he did but the sensations passing through him at her touch were too pleasurable. It had been a long time since anyone had touched him like this. A long time since anyone had cared. Still, there were more pressing matters requiring his attention. Matters like the deadly beastie coiled before him.

"Have you a weapon? A tool?" he asked, preparing to make sure the snake never got a chance to harm her.

"What for? You aren't thinking you're going to kill it. We're going to get this guy into this plastic bucket and put the lid on it."

She grabbed the bucket she intended to use, but he took it from her. If anyone was going to get bitten—again—he intended that it should be him.

"The only thing we have up here that even remotely resembles a weapon is Jebediah Toliver's civil war sword over in the museum office," she said with a chuckle as she stretched around to watch him. "I seriously doubt our little friend here would wait for me to run and get that even if we did want to cut his head off. Which we don't."

Iain wanted to give her a reassuring smile, but the coiled menace in front of him demanded his full attention. Sallie was watching too closely to miss it if the snake should bite him again. Explaining a disappearing snakebite was one conversation he didn't particularly want to have with her tonight.

Once he'd managed to trap the creature, she slapped a lid on top.

"There are already little holes in this lid. I was using it to strain pebbles out of the water." She grinned up at him as if they'd just shared an exciting moment. "I can't believe we found a rattlesnake up here. It's the first one I've seen in the four years I've been here. I'll call Animal Control and see if Skip can come out to pick it up tomorrow. Wow. Guess we'd better warn everyone to be extra-careful from here on out."

With the bucket safely settled in the corner, Iain hoisted the feed sack onto his shoulder and followed her from the shed to dump the grain into the feeder. A comfortable silence settled over them as they finished feeding and watering all the animals.

Once they'd secured the area, Iain trailed along beside Sallie as she headed toward the sleeping quarters.

In the silence that continued to stretch between them, he heard a soft sound from behind, like a boot sliding on loose gravel. Slowing his gait, he allowed himself to fall a step behind Sallie and then dropped to one knee, head bent to listen.

"What's wrong?" Sallie asked, turning as she apparently realized he was no longer at her side.

"Pebble in my boot," he said quickly, straining to hear into the dark that had fallen around them.

Someone was out there. Someone who watched and listened.

"Do you need help?" she asked.

He shook his head. What he needed was silence, but he could hardly say that aloud.

"Okay, then." She worried her teeth at the edge of her bottom lip, looking from him back into the direction they'd been headed. "If you don't need me, I'm going to take off. We have our first load of visitors coming up the mountain tomorrow and I still have to finish the final schedules before I get to bed tonight. And call Skip to see if he can come out get and our little visitor."

"Go," he said, flashing a smile to soften the edge of his response. "Tend to yer duties. I think I'll stay out here for a while and enjoy the quiet of the evening."

"Okay," she said again. "I'll have assignments posted before breakfast. As I've explained, you'll be shadowing me on the tours I lead tomorrow so you can start getting your feet wet. Go ahead and stay out as long as you like, but don't forget to keep your distance from the river. It's pretty dark over there since the fence and the lights got washed out. Good night, Iain."

"Good night, Sallie," he said, rising to stand as she walked away.

The only sounds reaching him now were those that belonged to the night. Damn his slow ears, anyway. He should have picked up on the noise before he had. He might have, too, if he hadn't been so focused on the time he spent with his lovely companion.

Any doubts he'd had earlier about her being the reason he'd been sent here were gone now. Learning that she had no family to watch over her had been the last piece of the puzzle falling into place. Sallie needed protecting and he'd been sent here to be her protector.

Iain stared into the shadows of the night, willing himself to see into the farthest reaches of the dark nooks and crannies, but it did no good. Whoever was out there, or had been out there, was either too well hidden or was gone by now.

With a sigh, he turned and headed toward the quarters where he slept. The bed he'd been assigned was comfortable enough but he had doubts about his ability to sleep tonight. There was a mystery afoot and far too much he didn't know.

Though one thing did stand out in the back of his mind. Dale, with his lies about having a relationship with Sallie, bore watching. Closely.

He pushed open the door to the sleeping quarters to be greeted by the warm glow of light. A moment later, Justin wandered in from the bathrooms, his face covered in white lather.

"Tomorrow it begins," Justin said with a chuckle. "Thought I'd at least start the season with a clean shave. If it's anything like last year, we'll get so busy soon that all I'll want to do at night is drop into bed, so who knows when I'll have the luxury of doing this again?"

Iain smiled a response, but didn't bother to answer as his co-worker disappeared back into the bathroom.

Instead, he threw back the blankets on his bed and admired the fine quality of the bedding as he had each night since he'd been here. Things had changed significantly since his day.

"Mind if I flip off the lights?" Justin asked as he came back into the room, wiping his face with a small towel. "We'll have to be up and at 'em early so I need to hit the sack."

"Not at all," Iain said, sitting down to remove his boots.

Once he sat on the soft bed, he realized just how tired he was. After the years he'd spent in limbo, exhaustion felt good. Everything he'd taken for granted his whole life, everything he'd been denied for the past two hundred years, felt good.

Being alive felt good.

"We kind of have a lights out early policy here once the season starts. If anyone wants to stay up and read or whatever, they can hang out in the food hall," Justin explained.

He padded over to the switch on the wall, but hadn't yet flipped it when the door swung open. Tony, Dusty and Dale came into the room, laughing.

"Oops," Tony said, shrugging sheepishly. "I forgot it's back to work routine. Sorry, Justin."

For his part, Justin simply arched an eyebrow and shut off the lights. "Either get here earlier or remember to carry your flashlights. As of opening day, sleeping quarters is for exactly that. Sleeping."

Iain rolled onto his back and pulled the covers up, his mind racing with all he'd encountered today. He'd never been one to jump to conclusions, but he strongly suspected that Dale was the one who had followed him and Sallie, both at the animal pens and in the mine that first day he'd been here. Tomorrow he'd see what he could learn to either prove his theory or eliminate the man from suspicion.

For tonight, however, he needed some rest. Though he didn't have any ideas what dangers Sallie would face tomorrow, he had no doubt there would be dangers. He had to be ready for anything that might come her way. It was the reason he was here.

She was the reason he was here .

CHAPTER FIVE

"Welcome, everyone, to the Toliver Mine. We're going to divide you into three groups in just a moment, but before we begin, I'd like to share just a few safety precautions that everyone needs to follow."

Sallie stood in front of the group of people who had filed off the train and down from the station to gather in front of the mine entrance. In Iain's view, she looked completely comfortable speaking to the crowd, in spite of her claims the night before about preferring the company of animals.

"The first thing to remember is keep an extra-close eye on your little ones. Our river is wildly beautiful and it tempts even the most cautious to draw near. But, its beauty masks its danger. We've had a particularly warm, wet spring here in Colorado and between the daily rains and the elevated snow-melt upriver, flooding has been a constant problem. As you can see, we lost our fencing to the last round of flooding and I can promise you, the banks of the river are loose and crumbly. It wouldn't take much weight at all to send the mud and anyone standing on it right down into the water." Her words were delivered calmly, but there was no doubt as to her seriousness. "We've placed logs in a line over there, to serve as a warning until the fencing company can get their crews out here. Don't cross over to the other side of the logs. Nothing on the other side is safe," she continued.

"Because if you fall in, we are definitely not coming in after you," Justin piped in as he joined her in front of the group, a big grin on his face. "You aren't getting out until the authorities fish your body out at the bottom of the mountain."

Annoyance flashed over Sallie's face, but it was gone so quickly, Iain wondered if anyone else had even noticed the expression.

"A little dramatic," Sallie said, glancing to her co-worker. "But a sad fact, I'm afraid. So, bottom line, keep everyone in your party away from the water."

Iain waited quietly for the visitors to divide themselves into three groups. Justin took the first group, Dusty the second, leaving the third for Iain and Sallie. He already knew from the explanations at breakfast that the three groups would start in different places so that only one group at a time would be inside the mine. He and Sallie started with the miners' shed, where Sallie went through a quick history lesson covering mining in general and what life was like for miners at the time.

In every training session, Sallie had stressed to him the importance of quickly learning about the group you led. Remembering each member of your group was the one way to recognize quickly if you'd lost anyone along the way. Their group consisted of one older couple, a large family group that appeared to be made up of a mother and father, grandparents and two children, a boy perhaps ten or eleven years old and a girl maybe six or seven. The group was rounded out with a couple who appeared to be in their late teens and another couple with a small boy, perhaps three or four years old.

Lots of little people to keep in mind as they wandered through the camp buildings and then into the mine.

Their group began in the miners' shed, where Sallie told them stories that highlighted what life for miners in any mine would have been like at the time.

Once they finished in the miners' shed, their group formed a line and trekked farther down the hill to the old mine office. Again, once everyone gathered, Sallie launched into a history lesson, this time covering facts that pertained specifically to the Toliver Mine. She kept things light and had the group laughing as she pointed out various items in the room that made the place as much a museum as a stop on the tour. The ornate sword hanging on the wall led Iain's thoughts back to the conversation he and Sallie had first thing this morning with Skip Harris, the Animal Control officer.

"Huh," the old man had said after peeking into the bucket. "I'm pretty sure that's a Massasauga rattler. I've seen photos, but never a live one. I pulled some info off the 'net last night after Sallie called me and described this little beauty. This species is native to Colorado, but not up here. You just don't find these babies above fifty-five hundred feet. Certainly not up here near ten-thousand. We'll have to think about where you came from, won't we, my lovely?" The officer had lifted the bucket when he spoke, grinning at Iain as he finished. "I like critters. They're downright fascinating to me. 'Specially ones like this that just plain don't belong where you find 'em. You mind if I keep the bucket?"

"It's yers," Iain had answered, already wondering how such a creature had found its way into Sallie's shed, considering all the Animal Control officer had told them.

Based on Skip's reaction, Iain suspected that someone might have put it there. But had their intention been that Sallie should be the one to find it? Maybe. All Iain knew for sure was that he was going to stay as close to her as possible. And later today, after the crowds were gone, maybe he'd do a little investigating to find out where Dale had been last night and what he'd been doing that had caused him to get into the dining hall so much later than everyone else.

Assuming he was still here to do that investigating.

Soni had sent him to save Sallie's life. Had Sallie been the one to lift that sack instead of him, she might not have survived the snake's bite. Although, had that been the event he'd been sent to change, the witch would already have come for him. Wouldn't she?

He had no more time to concentrate on that question. It was their group's turn to head into the mine. They made one last stop at the old ore cart that had been filled high with hard hats in a variety of colors to allow each guest to find one they'd be comfortable wearing.

"A couple more things before we go inside," Sallie was saying as Iain arrived at the back of the group. "Like everywhere else we've been today, you need to stay together. There's electric lighting along the main path when we get inside, but there are secondary tunnels leading off like a maze, and they're all as dark as the original mine. Those tunnels have barricades to warn you to stay out and for good reason. They aren't tourist-proofed, so we don't want anyone getting lost down there. Also, keep in mind that it's about fifteen to twenty degrees cooler inside, so if you have jackets or sweaters, you might want to put them on now."

"Thank goodness," the grandmother said to a burst of chuckles from the group. "I'm looking forward to some cool!"

As they made their way into the tunnel, the guests peppered Sallie with questions, all of which she answered efficiently and often with humor.

Iain recognized the side tunnel he'd wandered into his first time in the mine and saw that the yellow caution ribbons were back in place, along with a wooden sawhorse to block the opening.

"Why can't we go down there?" the older boy asked, pointing in that direction.

"Too dangerous," Sallie answered, pulling her flashlight out of her pocket and focusing its beam down the dark tunnel. "What you can't see from here, around the bend in that tunnel, are some boards lined up on the ground. A long time ago, some of the men working that tunnel drilled a shaft down there. They slanted it at a really sharp angle, figuring they just might be able to tap into the vein of silver that ran through the neighboring claim."

"Sounds illegal as hell," one of the men commented.

"It probably was," Sallie agreed. "But it wasn't the law that gave them their comeuppance. After a few hundred yards, the shaft flooded and there was a cave-in. Once they finally managed to escape, they boarded up the hole. But it's still there and still every bit as dangerous as it was then."

"Did anyone get killed when they had the cave-in?" the boy asked.

"Cameron!" his little sister objected, but she pushed around him, looking up at Sallie with huge eyes. "Did they? Are there ghosts in here with us?"

Sallie shook her head, matching the child's serious expression. "Luckily, everyone survived the cave-in. But shortly after, one miner was lost when he fell into the hole. That's why it's boarded up to this day and the passageway barricaded."

"So, are there ghosts?" the child asked again. "There are, huh?"

"That's a dumb question, Kelsey," her brother said, but he appeared to be waiting for an answer, too.

"Some people say that ghosts do walk these passageways," Sallie said, bending down to the little girl's height and smiling broadly. "But I doubt it. Ghosts aren't real."

"Oh, but they are," Iain blurted out, wishing he could pull the words back as soon as he spoke and all heads turned his direction.

"I knew it," Kelsey said, sidling closer to her brother and reaching for his hand. "Are they bad ghosts?"

Iain glanced toward Sallie to find her frowning at him. Obviously, he needed to handle this delicately, though he could hardly back out now that he'd started.

In for a penny, in for a pound, as the saying went.

"There's at least one ghost here in the mine. But I can personally guarantee you that he's no' bad. As a matter of fact, his whole purpose in being here is to see to yer safety. He'd give his own life to see you make yer journey safely back to the surface."

"But, wait," Kelsey said, dropping her brother's hand to come closer to Iain, propping her little hands on her hips and tilting her head to one side, in exactly the way Iain had seen many a grown woman do. "If he's a ghost, he doesn't have a life to give, does he?"

Bright child.

"Aye, wee lassie, you've the right of that. But that's what makes him work so hard to keep you from harm. You see, without a life to give, it's his very soul at risk if anything happens to you while yer here under his protection."

Kelsey thought for a moment and then a big smile spread over her face. "In that case, I'm glad that ghost is here. I'm even okay with being down here in the dark."

"Me, too," Sallie said, the frown that had wrinkled her brow slipping back into her customary smile.

Following along behind the group, Iain sighed. It had never been in his nature to keep secrets any more than it had been in his nature to be anything less than honest. That made it all the more important to face the fact that if he was going to be here much longer, he might need to work on learning to keep his mouth shut before he said too much. Either that or confess everything to Sallie.

Both avenues felt equally impossible.

Sallie stirred in him feelings, emotions he'd never known before. When she glanced back at him over the heads of the children who followed her and gifted him that smile she wore now, his whole heart felt as if it were twice as large as it was supposed to be. She was unlike any woman he'd ever met. A woman like this, a man could get lost in. A woman like this, a man could spend a lifetime loving.

If only he'd met her in another time, under other circumstances.

But he hadn't. He'd met her now, for only a single purpose and for only a very short time.

Somewhere down the line, he'd have to tell her the truth about who he really was and what he was doing here. He just didn't know how to do that yet. At least, not without risking the loss of that smile she cast his way.

CHAPTER SIX

Iain MacIntosh was one seriously impressive man.

Sallie tried to keep a smile off her face as she watched him collecting hardhats from all the guests who had been on their tour. Clearly, every one of them was just as enamored with him as she was.

There had been a moment there, back in the mine, when she'd had a concern that his unplanned response about ghosts was going to go very wrong. It wouldn't have taken much to frighten those children, upset their parents, and net themselves a slew of bad reviews that could have put a serious dent in their summer business.

But that hadn't been at all what had happened. Instead, Iain had charmed the lot of them, weaving a story as if he had personal knowledge of a ghost wandering the tunnels. It was such a good addition, in fact, she'd have to give some consideration to adding it to all the tours as a regular bit. If that was okay with Iain.

His deep chuckle reached her ears and she turned to find him lifting the little girl in their group to allow her to drop her hardhat into the bin with all the others. He was a gem, all right.

Easy on the eyes, easy on the ears, and easy on the mind. No wonder Nancy Toliver had hired him on the spot.

"Where's Markie, Don? I thought you had him with you."

The timbre of panic in the woman's voice jerked Sallie from her pleasant reverie.

Markie? The youngest member of their tour group had gone missing.

"Markie Glen!" the woman yelled. "You get away from there this instant!"

Sallie swiveled to look in the direction the woman faced. Her stomach knotted the instant she spotted him, scrambling over the logs that acted as an inadequate barrier to the river's edge.

She didn't hesitate.

Breaking into a full-on run, she raced toward the child, vaulting over the barrier to grab him in her arms only an instant before the water-soaked ground began to crumble beneath her feet.

No time to escape. No time to think. Only a split second to shove Markie back in the direction of the barrier before Sallie found herself falling into the cold clutches of the raging river below.

* * *

Iain saw Sallie run toward the river and matched his steps to hers. He knew deep in his gut she was in trouble even before the ground gave way beneath her. He *felt* it. This must be the moment he'd been sent here to prevent.

The moment he'd waited for. The moment he'd come to dread.

Without thought for his own safety, Iain plunged into the water after her, finding that luck had played in his favor for a change.

The shoulder of her shirt had caught on the twisted metal remains of the fencing she'd pointed out to him before. Caught, but not securely. Even as he reached for her, the cloth split into threads, giving way under the insistent pressure of the water battering against them.

Relief filled her eyes as his hand tightened around her wrist and he pulled her toward him. If only he could use both his hands! If only he could clutch her to him to prove to himself she was unharmed. But letting go of his tenuous hold on the pole that had stopped him from being carried off by the current was impossible.

She fisted her free hand in his shirt as she neared him and he drew her close. So intense was the connection between them, he could swear he felt her heart pounding against his chest as he held her. It would be so easy to get lost in those eyes. So easy to crush her lips against his to prove to himself that she was really in his arms, safe.

Only problem was, she was still far from safe.

The waters raged around them, tearing at their bodies, battering them with all manner of objects picked up and carried along by the floods. Sallie would be covered in cuts and bruises, he had little doubt. Already, blood streaked her shoulder where the metal had gouged into her skin as she'd been caught on the fencing. He hadn't the time to assess the damage right now. Any wounds she'd suffered were a small price to pay for the bent poles having held her long enough to allow him to reach her.

As much as he hated the thought of letting her go, he had to get her out of this river. He shoved her in the direction of the water's edge where she grappled for a hold, not yet close enough to reach. Only a few inches more and she'd be able to grab on to something to buy her time until someone from the ground above could help her.

"Iain!" she screamed, her eyes filled with panic as she let go of the bank to turn, to tug at his hand that clamped tightly around her wrist.

Too late he saw the fast approaching branch, driven by the water as if it were a spear thrown by an enemy. He managed to angle his body to shield her, but that was the best he could do. Pain seared through his chest and into his back. Pain such as he'd felt only once before, on a long-ago battlefield when the shot that had killed him tore into his head.

With a tremendous effort, he gave Sallie one last shove, forcing her to the water's edge where she clung to the remains of the twisted fencing at the foot of the bank, gulping sobs as she frantically grappled for his hand.

It took everything he had to move through the pain. Everything he had in him to pull away from her in order to maintain his hold on the twisted pole. Everything he had to keep from being swept under the water.

"Iain!" Sallie called out, her voice wavering over the sounds battering his ears.

With Sallie out of immediate danger, he could afford to assess his own situation. The branch, as large in diameter as a grown man's fist, protruded from his chest. The pain lancing through his body could easily have convinced him that he was truly among the living again. The lack of blood when he managed to pull it out told him otherwise. Just because he could feel pain and experience the emotions of a living man didn't mean he was alive.

He was indeed the ghost he'd spoken of in the mine.

Sallie screamed again as he pulled the branch from his chest and then she went eerily silent as he tossed it away into the churning water.

"Hold on, you guys," Justin yelled from the high bank. "We've got a rope now. Just hold on!"

A moment later, the end of the rope dropped down to Sallie's hands and she was being lifted up to safety.

Her eyes, though, were fixed on him.

Iain would never be able to erase the horror reflected there as she stared at the spot just below the water's level where the hole gaped in his chest. She'd seen, he had no doubt. Seen the hole. Seen the lack of blood.

There was no longer any question about what came next in his relationship with Sallie. He'd have no choice but to tell her the truth about who and what he was.

Assuming, that is, the witch allowed him to stay long enough to tell her. After all, he'd done what he'd been sent here to do. He'd saved her life. His task here was over. He'd earned his way to the promised land and his turn to have his revenge on Prince Charlie. It was all he'd wanted for over two hundred seventy years and now that moment was within his grasp. He should be the happiest man on the face of the planet.

So why did he feel so empty?

CHAPTER SEVEN

"You should have given this work to one of the others." Iain waited until Sallie lowered the grain bucket and turned to look at him. "Especially after all you've gone through today. Straining could easily break open the wound upon yer shoulder."

It was a sensitive subject, but one he had to address. The sooner the better. Now that she was safe, he'd likely not have much more time with her. If he was going to tell her the truth, he would have to do it now or never.

Her eyes pierced him, like a woman trying to crawl inside his head to find the answers she needed. Answers he had sworn to himself to give to her tonight.

"What happened out there today?" she asked, her voice barely more than a whisper.

If he were smart, he'd stay right where he was. He'd tell her what he needed to and then he'd walk away. If he were smart.

But *smart* wasn't the feeling in either his brain or his heart at the moment. It was *need* that consumed him now.

A need to console the vulnerable beauty standing only feet away from him. A need to feel her in his arms.

As foolish as it was, giving in to that desire was more powerful than any rational thought he'd ever experienced.

In three steps he was standing next to her. His body controlled him now, not his head. *Smart* had no place in his world at this moment. He wrapped her in his arms, his chin resting on the top of her head.

"Doona fash yerself over what happened today, lassie."

Given the choice, he would have spent the rest of his life as he was at this moment. But the choice was not his.

Sallie pushed away from him, her eyes searching his as she stepped back, leaving a hole as big and as empty as the one that had been in his chest while he was in the water.

"I know what I saw in that river, Iain. You can give whatever excuse you want to the EMTs or the rest of the staff. You can accuse me of being overcome and distraught with terror like everyone else did. But I know what I saw. We both know."

She had been frantic in the aftermath of the accident this afternoon. In spite of her own injuries, she'd run to him when they'd at last pulled him from the water, her hands searching his chest, her fingers ripping at the tear in his shirt, hunting for any sign of the wound she'd seen.

Of course, no sign of the injury had remained. A ghost could hardly be wounded any more than a dead man could be killed.

"All I want is the truth," she said, her voice tinged with the hurt he'd seen in her eyes as Justin had pulled her off him and carried her away.

"Then it's the truth you shall have," Iain answered softly, reaching down to lift the heavy bucket she'd carried. "Upon my oath. But I warn you, it's no' a pretty story. Nor is it likely to be one you'll easily accept. If I'm to tell it, I'll need to begin at the beginning."

"The truth," she repeated stubbornly. "All of it. From the beginning."

"So be it," he answered. "Before I do that, though, I need to tell you that I'll be leaving soon. I canna say with any certainty when, only that it will be soon."

He'd done what he'd been sent to do. The witch would no doubt be coming for him at any moment. His hope now was that he'd be able to give Sallie the explanation she deserved before he had to leave her.

"Why are you leaving?" She waited, hands on her hips, head defiantly tipped to one side, that tail of lovely brown hair swinging seductively over her shoulder. "Is it because of what happened in the river? I saw that branch pierce your body. I saw the hole it left when you pulled it out. I could have fit my whole hand inside that hole and yet, when you came out of the water, your skin was unmarked, as if nothing had ever happened. Why weren't you bleeding?"

The truth. He'd sworn to give it to her.

"Because dead men don't bleed."

Sallie took another step back from him, her eyes as wide as if she'd been slapped.

"What?" She blinked rapidly, her brows wrinkling toward one another. "What kind of ridiculous answer is that supposed to be?"

"The truth," he said with a shrug. "It's simple enough. I'm a ghost, Sallie. I know what I'm telling you is hard to believe, but it's the truth. I died from a gunshot to the head on the fields of Culloden Moor in 1746."

"Right." She breathed in deeply, slowly, the eyes that had been wide, narrowing as her expression hardened. "You died in 1746. Oh, you're priceless, Iain. Absolutely priceless. I guess the word *truth* in your vocabulary means the exact opposite of what it does in mine. Give me that bucket."

She tried to take it from him, but he held it out of her reach.

"The truth is the truth," he said. "In any vocabulary."

Her hands were back on her hips, her expression hard, perhaps even hurt. "Okay, then. So, let's say I accept your ridiculous story that you're a ghost." The roll of her eyes conveyed her lack of belief in spite of her words to the contrary. "What are you doing here? How did you get here from…from…Heaven or hell or, wherever it is you've been since…what was it? Three hundred years ago when you were supposedly killed?"

"Two hundred seventy years," he corrected quietly. "More or less. The entirety of those years spent in limbo, trapped on the same dreary battlefield where I and my compatriots were betrayed. Trapped on the same battlefield where my life was taken from me."

"And you've come here because…"

Time to tell her the whole of it.

"I dinna lie when I spoke to this before. I am on a quest of sorts. I'm here because, after spending centuries consumed with hatred for the man who was responsible for my death, I've been given a chance to take my revenge. An opportunity to settle the debt that chained me to this world. All I had to agree to do was to perform one wee task to convince the witch who held my fate in her hands that I was worthy of that opportunity."

"Okay, wait a minute. A witch? So now it's a ghost *and* a witch that makes your story possible." Sallie shook her head, her anger flashing in her eyes. "Don't leave me hanging at this point, Iain. What is this amazing task that you've come to perform?"

All the rest had been difficult. This would be the worst. He could feel her emotions billowing off her as it was. But, he'd promised her the truth. All the truth.

"My task was to save the life of an innocent. You. And now that I've done that, I expect Soni will be sending me on to take my revenge against Prince Charlie."

Sallie's mouth opened and closed once, twice, a third time before she managed to speak.

"That would be Bonnie Prince Charlie, I assume?" she said at last.

"No' so bonnie from where I stood," Iain grumbled. "But, aye, that is the man of whom I speak. The man who betrayed us. Who ran away, tail between his legs, to live out the life his cowardice and incompetence denied us."

She stared at him in silence, arms crossed in front of her. After what felt like an eternity, she reached out one hand.

"Give me the bucket, Iain." When he complied, she shook her head, all anger faded from her expression, leaving nothing but a sorrow such as he'd rarely seen. "Go away. I don't care where. I just don't want you here with me. Not if you can't tell me the truth. I think I deserve better than your made up little fairy tale."

"It is the truth."

She turned her back on him, walking away with a finality that cut him to the quick.

He should have expected as much. There had been a time, his time, when he wouldn't have believed such a story any more than she believed him now.

With a sigh drawn from the depths of his soul, he headed away from her. Away from the hurt and sorrow he hadn't the power to fix. Away from the empty eyes that had once held a sparkle of life that had seemed to come directly from Sallie's heart.

For just an instant, he caught himself wishing he could restore that spark. He wished he could do something to wipe away the hurt she wore like a funeral cloak. He'd give anything to see her happy again. Anything.

"Rubbish," he muttered under his breath, picking up the speed of his steps.

What did it matter to him, her obvious feeling of betrayal. He'd done nothing but save her life. She meant nothing to him.

"End this!" he demanded of the empty night sky. "Show yerself, Soncerae, and let me be done with this torture."

He waited, but the witch didn't show herself. Neither did she remove him from his current surroundings. Apparently, saving Sallie's life wasn't enough to win her favor. Apparently, he needed to suffer more. To continue to prove himself worthy.

A glance back toward the animal pens revealed nothing more than darkness. Sallie had moved on to the other side of the sheds. Maybe he should go back to her. Maybe he should try once more to explain…

He shook his head and turned again down the path to the lunch hall, doing his best to harden his heart.

What she believed was of no matter to him. He'd likely be gone from this place within hours, anyway. His only purpose in coming here was to save her life and he'd done that. Her happiness wasn't part of the bargain any more than his was. She wasn't his responsibility.

Now, if he could only convince himself that was true, perhaps he wouldn't feel as if he'd just lost everything that had ever mattered to him.

* * *

So much for her believing that she'd completely changed. So much for her having learned her lesson about men.

Sallie dumped the bucket she carried with much more force than she'd intended, splashing water in all directions. The goats were completely unimpressed, casting a reproachful look in her direction before returning to their feed.

To think she'd been close to hysterical with worry over that man.

She dropped the bucket at her feet and hung her head, eyes closed.

To think she'd almost allowed herself to imagine she might be falling for him. Iain. The gorgeous, soft-spoken, caring man who was likely a lunatic. Either that or an out-and-out liar.

Then again, considering her track record with men, falling for someone like him made perfect sense.

Thank goodness she found out before it went any further.

She bent to retrieve her bucket from the ground and straightened, taking a moment to wipe her eyes before she finished bringing water to the others.

When she heard the noise behind her, her anger sparked again, pushing aside all the self-pity.

"Go away, Iain. I told you, I don't have anything else to—" But it wasn't Iain standing behind her when she turned. "Dale. What are you doing out here?"

"So," he said, as if that one word carried the whole of his argument. "Who's the crazy one now?"

"Go away, Dale," she said, turning to finish her chores.

She hadn't the strength for another encounter with yet another crazy man tonight.

"I don't think so, Sallie," he said, stepping so close she could see the determined gleam in his eyes. "I need you to know that I'm the one you belong to. I'm the one who loves you. Not that crazy foreigner."

She was seriously not in the mood for this. Not tonight. Not when her heart already hurt. Or maybe she was. Maybe a fight to clear the air was exactly what she needed.

"Really, Dale? You're the one who loves me?" She snorted her derision. "Then what happened to you when I fell in the water? I saw you there with everyone else just before I fell. But it wasn't you who jumped in to save me, was it? No, it was Iain. You weren't even there to help everyone else pull us out. You were gone, completely, like you thought someone might expect you to risk your own precious butt."

His chin quivered and his expression hardened, the combination so potent she took a step back from him. A step he followed, ending up even closer to her than he had been before.

"None of that matters now. You're safe. You came through that just fine, because you were meant to. But your accident convinced me that we don't have any time to waste. Life is too precious. I'm done with waiting for you to realize what's standing right in front of you. I'm the man you need. You belong to me."

"You want to know who the crazy one is, Dale? Both of you." She poked a finger at his chest, hoping he'd back away. "I don't belong to anyone but myself. I don't need any man. And if I did, I can promise, it sure wouldn't be you."

Instead of moving away, he came closer, his presence overwhelming her. His hand snapped out, grabbing her wrist so quickly she didn't have a chance to dodge away. He pulled her close to his chest, pinning her injured arm behind her and dipping his head to within a fraction of an inch from her face.

"You're wrong, and I'm going to prove it to you. I should have thought of it for myself. But now I know. And when I'm finished with you, you won't believe there was ever a time you didn't want me."

He lifted her from her feet, forcing her face into his shoulder where she fought to catch her next breath. With each of her struggles, he increased the pressure on her injured arm until her vision dimmed with the pain.

He carried her, his hold effectively eliminating any possible chance of escape. She'd never imagined him to be so much stronger than her. As she struggled against him, she felt the wound on her arm break open, felt the moisture against her skin as blood soaked her shirt. Pain clouded her judgment, preventing her from forming any coherent plan of action. She had to do something to get away, but her options at the moment were clearly limited. Fighting wasn't a consideration as long as Dale continued to apply pressure to her arm. Even screaming was out of the question, as tightly as her face pressed into his chest.

All she could do was bide her time, hope he would come to his senses, and wait for the first opportunity.

The sliver of hope she'd been clinging to evaporated when Dale finally set her on the ground and she realized where they were. Deep inside the Toliver Mine, far down the sealed off tunnel where nobody ever came.

"Maybe we'll just tie up those wrists of yours," he said, grinning as he slipped off the shirt he wore. "Take a little of that willful fight out of you."

One look at Dale's face in the glow of the candle he'd lit and Sallie's hopes sank even lower. Whatever thin grasp on normal the man had held before tonight, it was completely gone now. She could really use a helping hand from the ghost Iain had invented on their tour.

If only Iain's ghost stories were real.

All of the stories he'd told her, stories about Faeries and witches and ghosts, flooded into her mind. As crazy as Iain had sounded with his claims of actually being a ghost, if she ever had the chance again, she'd happily take that kind of crazy over the lunacy standing in front of her right now.

If she ever had the chance again…

CHAPTER EIGHT

Light spilled out around Iain as he opened the door to the lunch hall. The delightful smells that met his nose reminded him of the evening meal he'd missed. His stomach rumbled in response and he took a plate from the stack. Might as well enjoy food one last time before he traveled on to the next stage of his journey.

Manda and Ashley were the only ones around, but they were busy in the kitchen, so, thankfully, he had no need to attempt conversation. He chose a table near the door, in case he needed to slip outside quickly. In spite of his hunger, the food felt heavy in his stomach, unwelcome. He found himself toying with the food, pushing it around on his plate, avoiding the next bite. What he needed was a cup of whisky. A large cup. Though, with the way his luck was going, the whisky would likely have no more effect on him than the snake venom had.

He dropped the fork to his plate and scrubbed his hands over his face.

Something just didn't feel right. Some little voice in the back of his head niggled at him, urging him to go back outside and find Sallie. Find her and give it one more go at explaining things to her before it was too late.

"Guess we were all wrong about those two," Tony said with a chuckle as he entered the room, Dusty following closely behind.

"Sure looked like it to me," Dusty agreed. "That's not something I ever thought I'd see, though. I guess we should let Justin know what's going on."

"Definitely," Tony agreed. "But I'm having some food first. I'm famished after spending the whole evening putting those picnic tables together."

Both men filled their plates and then joined Iain at his table.

"You are never going to believe what we just saw," Dusty said around his first bite.

"What are you?" Tony asked. "Some old woman? Damn, man. Gossip much?"

Dusty shrugged, stuffing his mouth full again. "He should know," Dusty said. "He's stuck with her until after his training is done. She might be coming on to him, too. Who knows?"

"What are you talking about?" Iain asked, a knot of concern building in his chest.

"Our new boss-lady," Dusty said. "We saw her making out with Dale over by the animal pens. Guess they thought it was too dark to be seen."

"This is going to cause trouble," Tony said, keeping his eyes fixed on his plate. "Nothing like this has ever happened in the whole time I've been here."

"Which is why old lady Toliver should have left Justin in charge when she took off for Europe." Dusty wagged his fork at his companions. "I'm telling you, this is what you get when you put a chick in charge."

"Where did you see them last?" Iain asked.

"Heading into the mine," Dusty said, his eyebrows waggling to match his leer. "Him carrying her in his arms. Looking for a little kissy-kissy time, if you get my drift."

Iain did indeed get the man's *drift*. He just wasn't accepting it. No matter how upset Sallie had been with him, there was nothing he'd seen, nothing he'd heard from her that would indicate she had in any way changed her mind about Dale.

He certainly hadn't. After the incident in the mine and finding the snake, Iain was more convinced than ever that Dale was a threat to Sallie. And now she was heading into the mine with him? Willingly?

He couldn't believe it. Wouldn't believe it.

Iain rose from his seat and headed out into the night, his steps increasing in speed as he neared the entrance to the mine. Just inside the opening, he stopped, tipping his head to the side to concentrate all his senses on discovering where Sallie was.

Nothing.

If Dale had indeed taken Sallie into the mine as Dusty and Tony said, he hadn't bothered to turn on any lights. Iain didn't care for the possibilities that omission suggested.

He moved out of the moonlit night and into the dark cavern. Once inside, he paused again, allowing his eyes time to adjust to the complete absence of light.

Except, complete absence of light wasn't what he saw as his eyes adjusted. A faint glow in the distance drew him forward. A faint glow outlining the entrance to one of the secondary tunnels. The very one, in fact, that he'd been drawn down his first day at the Toliver Mine.

Quietly, quickly, he made his way down to the opening, following the light inside. He found them exactly where he'd suspected—where he'd feared—he would, beside the boarded-up shaft that was the reason this tunnel had been closed off.

Only the shaft wasn't boarded-up now. The cover had been removed, the hole gaping open, dark and threatening like some giant mouth waiting to be fed.

No wonder Soni hadn't come for him after he'd pulled Sallie from the water. He hadn't yet done what he'd been sent here to do.

Like an animal of prey stalking its kill, Iain paused, assessing the scene before him. He needed to take his time. No quick actions that could create a greater risk of harm for Sallie. This situation required that he use his cunning and stealth to determine the best plan of attack.

Dale, bare-chested, stood over Sallie, his face a maniacal mask of glee. She lay curled on her side on the ground, her hands bound together in front of her. She was alive, though it was clear from her expression, she was terrified. That alone was almost enough to push Iain over the edge. When she tried to sit up, tried to scoot away from her captor, Iain saw the large splotch of fresh, wet blood staining her shirt. All rational thought escaped him, leaving only a red haze of fury to blanket his mind.

A snarl of rage passed over his lips as he charged Dale. They both hit the rock floor with a sickening *thud*, the smaller man gasping in pain beneath him. Iain didn't care. He wanted to hurt Dale. Wanted to make him pay for what he'd done to Sallie. He smashed his fist into the other man's face before rising and lifting Dale to his feet, only to send him reeling back to the floor with another explosive punch.

Somewhere in the deep recesses of his mind, some small part of Iain was aware he'd lost all control, but that didn't matter to him now. Nothing mattered except his need to make sure Dale never harmed Sallie again.

Only when Sallie's screams pierced his consciousness did he finally stop.

She huddled near the wall, her eyes giant saucers of fear. It took little imagination for him to realize that her fear was as much his doing as it was Dale's.

"By all that's holy," he muttered, releasing his hold on the man's neck.

Dale's body crumpled to the floor and Iain stepped over him to help Sallie rise unsteadily to her feet.

Some fine savior he'd turned out to be. He'd shown himself to be as much of a beast as Sallie's attacker had.

He pulled her close and wrapped his arms around her, muttering the same mindless soothings to her as he remembered his mother saying to him when he was a small child awakened by nightmares. Within his embrace, she shivered, as if overcome with the cold.

She needed warmth and light. She needed medical attention for her shoulder. As much as he might wish to remain here forever, her locked in his arms, he needed to get her out of this place.

With an arm to the back of her knees, he lifted her from her feet, reveling in the feel of her so close to him. It was as if she were a part of him. As if she belonged here next to him. When she locked her arms around his neck and nuzzled her head into his shoulder, he spared another thought to staying here in this very spot, just like this, for all eternity.

But of course, that was mere fantasy.

A fantasy that shattered into a million pieces as he heard the slow hand clapping behind him.

"Now there's a sight I never expected to find," Justin said. "What a strange little twist to our play."

Iain turned to find Justin several feet away, his face a mask, devoid of any emotion. As unnerving as the picture he presented, it was the old sword which had hung in the museum office clutched in one hand that drew Iain's attention.

"It was the only weapon I could find up here," Justin said with a chuckle. "But don't let the age of the steel fool you. I made sure it was sharp and deadly, just in case, you know."

"Just in case, what?" Iain asked, slowly lowering Sallie to her feet.

"Just in case a moment like this presented itself," Justin said, twirling the weapon in front of him. "Just in case I had the opportunity to eliminate my competition. Like I do now."

"Competition?" Sallie said, her voice quivering as her body trembled. "What are you talking about?"

"You, of course," Justin answered. "You stole my promotion. My raise. I've been here as long as you have. I was the one who should have been made manager, not you."

"This is about Nancy having promoted me instead of you?" Sallie shook her head, taking an unsteady step forward. "But I thought you were cool with the idea. You never said anything."

"Like it would have done any good to have said anything after that old biddy decided to put you in charge?" Justin's laugh lacked all humor. "No, you put some kind of spell on her. Wound her around your little finger and stole what should have been mine. Well, I'm putting things to rights tonight, just like I planned from the beginning."

With the sword held out in front of him, Justin advanced until he could push at Dale's limp body with his foot, eliciting a weak groan from the other man.

"What is it you planned to do to us?" Iain asked, edging forward a step.

His best hope was to maneuver himself in between Justin and Sallie so that he could provide a barrier when Justin chose to act.

"You weren't supposed to be a part of this at all, Iain." Justin shook his head, a sad smile lifting one corner of his mouth. "I actually feel kind of bad about that. But, oh well. Your bad fortune to be in the wrong place at the wrong time. Maybe it's for the best, you coming down here after Dusty told you about Sallie and Dale. The cops will assume it was some lover's triangle gone wrong when they find your bodies."

"Our bodies?" Sallie squeaked, taking another step toward Justin. "You can't be serious. No job is worth hurting people."

"I'm not going to hurt you, boss-lady," Justin said, using his foot to shove one of Dale's legs over into the gaping hole next to where he lay. "I'm going to eliminate you."

"You won't get away with this," Sallie warned, but Justin only laughed.

"Of course I will. I'll admit, things haven't gone as smoothly as I had hoped, but it's all different now. This time there won't be any screw-ups."

"That first day I arrived," Iain said, hoping to distract Justin. "You were the one here in the tunnel. You were the one calling Sallie's name."

Justin nodded, followed by a shrug of one shoulder. "But you were the one who heard and came looking, not her. I knew then, I needed a better plan."

"Like a poisonous snake?" Iain asked, finally putting the pieces together.

"Exactly." Another chuckle and shake of his head. "But that didn't work, either. So this time I decided I wasn't taking any chances. I would deal with the situation myself. Hands on, so to speak."

Beside him, Sallie took another step forward, as if completely oblivious to the danger in front of her. Slowly, with as little obvious movement as possible, Iain snaked his arm behind her and hooked one finger into her belt loop. She was already too close to that monster.

"I can't believe you'd ever consider doing something like this," she said.

"Believe it," Justin snapped, his eyes flashing his anger. "I was tired of something always saving you. So today, I came down here and opened the shaft. And then I found Dale and told him that I'd seen you and our big Scot here down by the stables, having a little romantic alone time. It was easy to see from the first day that he liked you. And once I made those pills he took every day disappear, it wasn't long before that turned into an obsession."

"I didn't realize Dale was on any medication," Sallie said.

"Guess that's another disadvantage you have in being a woman. You weren't living in the same quarters with him. I saw and I asked about them. Once I knew he had a problem, it didn't take much to know what being without them would do. I simply planted a couple of ideas. I told him I'd heard you telling one of the girls you had this fantasy about some big, strong man bringing you down here. About how you wouldn't be able to resist a man who did something like that. I knew he'd bring you here. All I had to do was wait for someone to tell me about it and then follow. It was a perfect set up. Him attacking you, you fighting back. Me finding the two of you, tragically, too late to stop what had happened. All of it ending with Toliver Mine in need of a new manager. That's where I come in."

With a grin, Justin used his foot to shove Dale one more time. The man on the floor grunted as his second leg slipped over the edge and dangled into the hole.

The effort left Justin off-balance for just a moment and, in that moment, everything happened at once.

"What have you done?" Sallie screamed, straining to run forward.

Only the thin strip of material in Iain's grip held her back. Until it gave with a ripping sound that tore at Iain's heart. The sword slashed through the air, slicing into Sallie's forearms as she lifted them to shield herself.

With a fury cry drawn from deep in his soul, Iain was airborne, leaping toward Sallie's attacker as she fell to the ground. Justin swung the sword around and up, puncturing into Iain's chest. The blade drove deep, piercing through muscle and bone as Iain threw himself into Justin.

Nothing so simple as a mortal wound could stop him. Not now. Not with Sallie's life hanging in the balance.

He charged forward, not stopping, fighting through the pain as the sword cut deeper still, its tip finding exit from his body through his back. He didn't stop until his hands closed around Justin's neck.

"What are you?" the other man managed to choke out before Iain's grasp tightened, strangling off his air.

"Naught but a ghost," Iain whispered in return, loosening his grip only when Sallie's screams brought him back to his senses.

As he released Justin, he shoved him backward, sending the man stumbling away from him, away from Sallie. Justin's feet slid in the loose gravel, his arms windmilling as he struggled to regain his balance. He might have, too, if it hadn't been for Dale's prone figure beside the shaft opening.

Iain ignored Justin's cry for help as he tumbled into the gaping hole, his full attention turned to Sallie. Blood soaked her shirt from the shoulder wound that had reopened in her struggles. It also dripped down her arms and into her lap from the slices into her forearms.

"Stay with me, my love," Iain murmured, dropping to his knees beside her. "We'll get you help."

"You'd better help you, first," she said weakly, pointing to the sword that still jutted from his chest.

How could he have forgotten? With both hands wrapped around the shaft of the weapon, he gave it a mighty tug and dislodged it from his chest, tossing it to the ground once it was out. He paid only the slightest attention to the fact that it hurt much less coming out than it had going in.

He gathered Sallie in his arms and rose to his feet, his only thoughts on how quickly he could get her out of the mine where she could receive the proper medical attention.

"You were telling the truth, weren't you?" she asked, her face wet with tears. "There's no blood at all, even though that sword should have killed you. You are a ghost, aren't you?"

"There's no' a need for you to fash yerself over such things now. We're going to get you out of here and all patched up, aye?"

"Don't leave me, Iain. I need you to stay here with me."

She pleaded with him as if the decision were his to make. He'd already told her the decision wasn't his. If it were up to him, he'd spend the rest of his days right here with her.

Behind him, Justin's cries abruptly silenced and an eerie green mist wafted around his knees. He'd seen such a mist before, each time the witch had taken one of the men from the battlefield.

"The time has come, Iain. You've saved the lass. You've proved yerself and earned yer reward."

Soni stood only feet away from him, the green mist swirling around her like a cocoon. A cocoon her extended arm invited him to join her inside.

"No' this very moment, Soni. Please," he said, tightening his hold on Sallie. "I've need of a bit of time. I've need to deliver the lass out of the mine. She's hurt and needs care. If I leave her here, I canna say when someone will find her to get her that help."

"That's no' yer responsibility, Iain. We'd a bargain, aye? Ye' were sent here to perform a task. Now that ye've done so, ye' must return to where ye are supposed to be."

* * *

It was all true! Every single word Iain had said to her. All true.

Sallie tightened her fingers in the cloth of Iain's shirt, determined not to let this woman in the mist, this witch, take him away from her. She'd fight for him, if only she didn't feel so light-headed.

"No!" she said, surprised when Iain started, as if he'd forgotten that he held her.

"Ye've no say in this, lass. It's Iain's destiny we discuss," Soni said, her arm dropping to her side. "The fulfillment of his dreams and desires."

But going with the witch wasn't his dream. At least it hadn't always been. He'd told her as much, himself, that first time he'd helped her feed the animals.

"No," Sallie insisted again, struggling to lift her head. "You may well be a powerful witch, but you don't know what his dreams really are. I do. He told me. He wants land and animals to tend. And one day, a family of his own. He can have all that if he just stays here. He doesn't need to go with you."

"Oh, but he does," Soni answered, lifting her cloak-shrouded arm toward him once more.

"Buy, why?" Sallie asked, hating that her voice cracked with the tears she wouldn't be able to hold back much longer. "Because he's dead? Because you have to deliver his soul somewhere?"

"The prince awaits your arrival, Iain. It's time for me to fulfill my part of our bargain," Soni said.

"No, leave him here. Give him a chance at all those dreams he had before he gave his life in battle," Sallie pleaded.

If only the dizziness would allow her some clarity of thought. Instead, she felt as if she viewed the whole scene unfolding around her through a shrinking window.

"We have to go now," Soni said, as if she'd heard nothing Sallie had said.

"At least allow me to carry her from the mine," Iain said, his voice sounding none too steady.

"Now, Iain." Soni repeated. "The prince is waiting."

Desperation tightened Sallie's throat until a sudden idea gave her new hope. "He's earned his chance at happiness by doing what you asked of him. If you must take someone with you, take me. Look at me," she held up one blood-streaked arm. "I'm close enough to being dead, right? Let him stay and have the chance he didn't have before. Take me instead."

"No!" Iain bellowed, his arms tightening around Sallie. "I'd choose the pits of hell before I'd allow that."

"Ye'd choose eternity in hell for the sake of this woman, would ye'?" the little witch asked, her voice faint as if coming from somewhere far away. "But would ye' give up that most dear to ye? Would ye' give up yer chance to have yer revenge?"

Sallie felt herself losing her battle with the darkness that closed in on her. She tried to speak, tried to hold on so that she could tell Iain how much she wanted him to stay. But it was too late for any of that as her grip on consciousness slipped away

CHAPTER NINE

"I think she's coming around at last, David. Should I get the nurse?"

Sallie struggled to open her eyes. Her brain swirled with a white fog of fluffy numbness that made it nearly impossible for her to sort out her thoughts. Was that her stepmother's voice she'd heard?

"Hey, baby-girl," a man who looked remarkably like her father said. He leaned over her, stroking her forehead. "You gonna wake up for us at last?"

He didn't just look like her dad. He actually was her father.

"Daddy?" she managed to croak.

It felt like someone had stuffed a dry sausage into her mouth where her tongue belonged.

"I'm here, baby-girl," he said, his rough fingers stroking gently against her cheek. "Netta is getting the nurse to let her know you're finally awake. You need anything?"

Answers. She needed answers. The last thing she remembered was that pretty little witch insisting that Iain had to leave her there in the mine. Had he gotten help for her? Had her co-workers found her?

"Where is...what happened to..." She struggled to form the questions that haunted her. "How did I get here?"

"Those kids you work with," Netta said, joining David at her bedside. "They got the sheriff out there and the ambulance and got you down the mountain to the hospital."

"They got those two men that hurt you, too." Her dad kept petting her head like he would a frightened animal. "And I know how soft-hearted you are, but I already told the authorities that we want the book thrown at them both. I don't care what their stories are or how sorry you end up feeling for them. They belong behind bars so they can't do this to anyone else."

No mention of Iain.

Sallie closed her eyes and wished that she could melt away, back in the white fluffy world she'd been floating in before. Back into the world where she'd had no ability to form words or thoughts. The very idea that Iain was gone was more painful than anything she had endured up to this point. Without him, her world felt bleak and empty.

"Anyone else?" she asked, without much hope.

"It was one of the girls at your work who called us. Ashley, I think. Your Dad and I got right in the truck and headed out the minute he got off the phone so we could be here for you. We already talked about you coming home while we were driving up here and we decided, well, you tell her David." Netta stepped back from the bedside, nodding toward her husband. "Go on. You tell her what you said to me."

David cleared his throat. Twice.

Sallie opened her eyes once more, surprised to find tears glistening on her father's cheeks.

"I was wrong, baby-girl. I should have never said that you had to leave home. I don't care what happened in the past. You belong back out on the ranch, with us, where we can keep an eye on you and make sure you're safe."

"That's what he said all on his own before we even got here," Netta added, her head bobbing up and down. "It wasn't any of my idea at all, Sallie. Your daddy was worried sick about you."

Sallie smiled in spite of the pain constricting her heart. Netta had always been on her side, even when her father had insisted that she needed to grow up. Netta had been the one cajoling her father to reconsider when David had insisted that the only way that Sallie would learn to make better choices was by relying on herself, not her family.

"It's okay, Dad," Sallie said at last. "I've got a good job here. I'm happy where I am."

At least, she had been. With Iain gone, the mine wouldn't be the same. Of course, without Iain in her life, it didn't matter where she was. One place was no better than any another.

A nurse bustled in, cheery and efficient, shooing everyone away from the bed so that she could check all the vital signs that held the story of how Sallie was healing.

"When can I get out of here?" Sallie asked.

Laying in this bed would only give her more time to think about how miserable she was.

"That's up to the doctor," the nurse said with a smile. "But, between the two of us, I'd be surprised if they kept you overnight again. You're going to be sore for a while, with all those stitches. But that's the case whether you're here or at home. I'm sure he'll just tell you to take it easy for a while."

Being sore, Sallie already knew about. It was the invisible wounds, the ones in her soul, that would take much longer to heal.

CHAPTER TEN

The long blare of the train whistle warned Sallie that she approached the station at Toliver Mine. She sat up straight in her seat and wiped her hands over her face, readying herself to face her crew. After a week away, she couldn't help but wonder what she'd find when she got there.

As it turned out, the nurse had been correct in her assumptions. The doctor had released Sallie from the hospital that same evening. Her father had insisted that, if she wasn't going to agree to come home with him and Netta, they would all stay in a hotel for a few days until he could satisfy himself that she was ready to return to work. He hadn't even allowed her phone contact with the people at the mine.

"The doctor said you could leave the hospital if you promised you'd rest," he'd said. "Worrying about work and trying to direct every little thing from your bedside isn't resting. They can handle it without you for a few days."

Her time away had morphed from a few days into a full week. If her father had his way, it would have been even longer. But, finally, Netta had convinced him that Sallie was doing more harm to herself worrying about what might be going wrong than she would by going back to work to see how well her staff had handled everything in her absence.

Sallie hoped her stepmother was right about things operating smoothly without her, but she had her doubts. She knew there was always more work than they could get done every day and that was when they were fully staffed. Operating smoothly when they were down four bodies? That would be a miracle.

She braced her shoulder against the seat as the train pulled to a stop, protecting her healing injuries from any unnecessary jostling. Putting stress on her stitches would only delay her recovery and keep her out of action that much longer. The platform was full of tourists, all waiting to take the last train of the day back down the mountain.

Dusty, Ashley and Tony gave her a wave, but kept their attention on their guests, assisting them onto the train and sending them off with the good cheer that everyone at Toliver Mine prided themselves in giving. It was that extra bit of attention that kept people coming back to the mine time and again.

It was reassuring to see that, although some things might have slipped while she was gone, her people had kept their focus where it was most important—on their customers.

There were so many things she needed to do. The tasks kept running through her head, tumbling over each other as to which deserved top spot on her list. She needed to check the schedule. Make sure tours were coordinated with the station master at the foot of the mountain. Check in with Manda to see whether they'd made a supply run since she'd been gone.

In spite of all the paperwork that waited for her in the office, her feet turned naturally to the one place she'd missed the most.

Above all else, she wanted to make sure her animals had been properly cared for in her absence. She didn't doubt they'd been fed and watered. But it wasn't the lack of food and water that concerned her. No one else here understood the importance of spending time with the animals. No one else understood that each of the sheep and the goats had their own individual personalities. They all wanted just a few moments of attention each evening. Even the llama needed a little extra love at the end of each day.

The sounds from the animal pens reached her ears long before she made her way around the stable. Not sounds of hunger or abandonment, but the normal, happy noises the livestock made when their dinner was being served.

She rounded the stable and came to a full stop, her heart pounding in her chest as she struggled to accept the scene in front of her.

He squatted on the ground, sheep on either side of him, scratching their heads as if they were big dogs. When he stood, he lifted a sack of feed on one shoulder, his path carrying him toward the llama pen.

How could it be?

"Iain?" she whispered, unable to move forward in her shock. And then more loudly, "Iain!"

He turned, the smile that so captured her heart, breaking over his face. The heavy sack he carried fell unnoticed to the ground as he started toward her, his jog quickly turning into a full-out run.

She grunted when he gathered her in his arms and pulled her close.

"I couldna' find you," he said, his voice little more than a breathless whisper in her ear.

"Me?" she said, wrapping her arms around his neck. "I thought you were gone. Why didn't you come to the hospital?"

"I did. The night you were taken there, I followed as soon as the sheriff was finished taking my statement. You were sedated when I arrived and they sent me home. When I returned the next evening, they told me you'd been released. I was in a panic when I got here and you were nowhere to be found."

He'd looked for her. He'd stayed here, and he'd tried to find her.

"My father insisted on a hotel."

"So I learned from Manda. She said yer father would allow none to interrupt yer recovery, so we none of us knew where to find you."

Sallie pulled back from him, her hands sliding to his cheeks while she studied his face. "The witch let you stay? In spite of your bargain with her?"

"Aye," he said, his grin returning. "She's a tricky one, that Soni. Drives a hard bargain, she does. Though, in some ways, I canna help but suspect she knew from the beginning what it was she expected of me."

As his words settled over Sallie, a new fear began to form.

"Does that mean that you'll still have to go? Will she be coming back for you?"

He shook his head. "No, she'll no' be returning."

"But what about the prince? What about your chance to have your revenge?"

Iain shrugged, his smile not wavering. "Giving that up was the price of Soncerae's final bargain with me."

He'd given up his chance at revenge? The one thing he'd told her he'd wanted for well over two hundred years? The one thing that had kept him going all that time?

"Oh, Iain, I'm so sorry."

She buried her head in his chest, but this time it was him who pulled back, his hands cupping her face.

"There's naught to be sorry for, Sallie. Giving up the chance to pummel a dead man is a small enough price to pay for a chance to spend a lifetime with the woman you love. If you'll have me, that is."

"A lifetime…" she echoed, trying to fully comprehend what it was he was telling her. "Me? You're in love with me?"

"Aye, yer the woman I love. And, thanks to Soni's determination to see me find my true happiness, I'm here for as long as you'll have me."

"I'll have you forever!" Sallie vowed, wrapping her arms around his neck again.

"Thank you," she whispered, hoping that, somehow, somewhere, Soni could hear her.

It may have been Iain's happiness the little witch had sought when she'd first sent him from Culloden. But in the process, she'd insured Sallie's happy ever after, too.

Dear Reader ~

Anyone who has read anything I've written likely knows that Scotland has long been a place close to my heart. I've invested hundreds of hours in research to attempt to stay as true to the actual history as possible in all my books. Never was this more in the forefront of my thoughts than while working on this story. Having known only the basics of the Battle of Culloden before preparing to write this story, I found my visits to Culloden Moor unusually moving and emotional. Knowing the history as I do now, I understand why.

Have a comment or a question? You can find me on Facebook at www.Facebook.com/Melissa.Mayhue.Author. Or, contact me directly at Melissa@MelissaMayhue.com. I'd love to hear from you! We even have a special Facebook group just for the readers of this series and lovers of all time travel romance. We'd love to have you join us - www.Facebook.com/groups/Magic.of.Time/.

If you enjoyed this book, please consider leaving a review at your favorite online retailer or at Goodreads.com to help other readers find it.

~ Melissa

ABOUT THE AUTHOR

MELISSA MAYHUE, married and the mother of three sons, lives at the foot of the Rockies in beautiful Northern Colorado with her family and one very spoiled Boston Terrier. In addition to writing *The Magic of Time* Series, she has also written two additional paranormal historical series, *The Daughters of the Glen* Series and *The Warriors* series. She is also writing *The Chance, Colorado* Series, contemporary feel-good romances set in a small mountain town.

Want to be notified when the next book is due out? Sign up for Melissa's new release newsletter at her website, www.MelissaMayhue.com.

Made in the USA
Las Vegas, NV
24 November 2021